AND IT RAINED *Blessings*

AND IT RAINED *Blessings*

Manisha Kanoria Lohia

RUPA

Published by
Rupa Publications India Pvt. Ltd 2022
7/16, Ansari Road, Daryaganj
New Delhi 110002

Sales centres:
Allahabad Bengaluru Chennai
Hyderabad Jaipur Kathmandu
Kolkata Mumbai

The views and opinions expressed in this book are the author's own. Names, characters, places and incidents are either the product of the author's imagination or are used fictitiously and any resemblance to any actual person, living or dead, events or locales is entirely coincidental.

ISBN: 978-93-5520-276-5

First impression 2022

10 9 8 7 6 5 4 3 2 1

Printed in India

This book is a dedication to my inner quest as a seeker, which has taken me closer to understanding the self and the larger fraternity of my fellows.

I lay this book at THE DIVINE LOTUS FEET *of my creator, my* GOD, *who has graced me with the flow of words.*

Contents

Preface

And It Rained Blessings is an inner expression of many special and silent moments I have experienced in the lap of nature. Unconsciously, the words have taken me into an inner realm, one I had never known before. As these words were woven into poems, I slowly started relating to the self within. Here are expressions related to aspirations, dreams, children, mischief, silence and God.

Writing has given me a beautiful inner world to tap into, a world which was otherwise unexplored. Through these poems I have discovered my own self as a human *being,* and not a human simply *doing*. Every poem here has brought me closer to identifying myself and brought me to the purpose of this life. There have been moments where I have been stunned after reading a poem I have penned down. The reason has been simply as I realized a higher force was writing through me. I understood that wherever there is love and passion, the creator chooses to act through us.

My extreme gratitude to my Matha, Pitha, Guru and Deivam, who have ignited the spark within me to express myself through these poems. This collection of poetry has been compiled during my online writing journey with Megha Bajaj over the last four years. She has shown me that words can become intoxicating when they flow as poetic expressions.

My obeisance to the revered Mahatria for making me believe in my own potential and drawing me closer and closer to my God.

God

G for Generator;
O for Operator;
D for Destroyer.
One of many interpretations for the word?

The experience of God is
So cleansing,
So purifying,
So energizing.
Can *he* ever be a destroyer?

For God means peace,
bliss, purity,
love personified,
a whirlpool of Energy!

In every experience of God
I am Meera, who
surrendered herself to
her Krishna's arms,
Dissolving her self in *him*.

The me, mine, myself
united with *him*.
As there was no self,

me merged with *ra,*
the rays of the sun.

A fragment of the nature of God.

God Is, God Alone Is!

The vastness of the sky,
the immensity of God.

The tenderness of the flower,
the warmth of a mother's touch.

The uniqueness of each leaf,
the special, the rare—me.

The waves of the sea,
the restless turbulent mind.

The rootedness of the trunk,
the firm faith and belief.

In this God is, God alone is
now, forever and for eternity!

Prayer

The sun shines
on a sunny day.
Birds fly
freely in the sky.

The flowers blossom
on a spring day.
Seeds sprout
as the tree begins.

The fountain flows
in the garden night.
Children play
in their parents' sight.

What beauty!
What joy!
As every form is right
in God's world, so very bright.

In all this we must pray,
connecting ourselves to our God,
expressing our love for all.

And in this, we shall never fall…

My God

One who lives within me
in every moment,
with whom I breathe,
with whom every heart beats,
who is He?
None other than God *himself.*

I have worshipped *him* in idols,
I have sought *him* through prayers.
Yet, I felt *him* not.
In vain, I realized
He had moved further away.

Until a moment arrived
where with *his* Grace,
I received *his* Grace.
And I felt *my* God
nearer than the nearest—
a Presence which carries me,
holds me, nurtures me.

He caresses my worries and
nourishes my dreams.
I forget myself, my attributes;
I lose myself unto *him.*
I feel the power as it comes

from *him,* and I feel complete.

The 'I' dissolves in *him;*
I merge with *him.*
There is no me,
there is no I.
He alone exists!
A Presence eternal
who is my God!

Aha! Children

They say after we are no more
embodied flesh and blood,
we become like stars—
lighting up the sky, adding
infinite beauty to the darkness
that surrounds the universe!

And children, aha children!
Do they not add infinite beauty
to our lives? Lighting everything
around and within us,
igniting the child within to spark.

Their smile, their touch,
their words; does it not feel like
God *himself* has descended on earth
to cast a magical spell
on each one of us
and transform in *his* spell?
I say, children are the most
sensitive of all beings,
spreading their innocence and charm
through all the lives they touch.
Leaving a trace of their purity
for us to become as divine.

Sitting near my window sill,
I admire the dark sky
with its immaculate beauty,
an array of shining stars...
An ever-longing desire arises
to become like them!
To be ever remembered
as myself...as I have learnt from
children, aha children!

Mother

A word, which associates itself
with unconditional love,
with forgiveness,
with immensity,
beyond one's own self,
to only think of what more...

Mother is synonymous to
what next!

Her love is as deep as the ocean,
the depths of which is unseen.
Her eyes encompass everything,
yet disclose nothing
but love and love alone!
Can any natural calamity
ever affect the ocean?
Can any turbulence
ever shake the love
that a mother possesses
for her child?

A love which is
as vast as the sky...
Incomprehensible,
inexplicable,

ever calm, ever peaceful.
The one who nurtures the child within
and bears the kicks and the pains—
yet ever calm, yet ever peaceful—
is a mother.

A Beautiful Within

Does the face reveal everything?
I often ask myself,
and in faith, I receive an answer
at an opportune time.

It all happened...
A divine experience of silence
in communion with my God;
I was only with *him*.

There was an inner urge
to purify what lay within,
to beautify and cleanse the core
and experience the divine within.

Like a male musk deer,
moves as a vagabond
to trace the smell of *his* origin.
But in vain, for it is emitted from within.

What is this search, O human?
Where art thou wandering?
Running, running, all the time
hither thither and neither!

End this search, O fleeting mind!
For the one is within,
we are all made in *his* image
to love and love alone.

He hath created us to create,
to think, to feel, to express, to be...
and in turn, to leave our footprints
On the sands of time...

Letting Go, Letting God In

I have learnt the art of letting go of things irrelevant;
I have learnt the art of living, of letting love in;
I have learnt the art of letting go, of living, loving and letting God in.

I am one with *him*...

Do We Need a Reason to Be Happy?

A phrase often heard—
do we need a reason to be happy?

I always say 'children'
in the true sense, because children
by their very nature are happy;
have you ever seen an unhappy child?

Always dancing and swaying,
thinking what next, what more?
Their minds in perpetual rhythm
of play, of movement, of fantasy.

I feel the happiest with children.
It ignites the spark within,
to skip, to dance, to do the craziest
things beyond comprehension.

To whirl like a child,
and go on endlessly.
To lose myself
and dissolve in the whirls.

The most beautiful of all
experience is to keep whirling,
till the mind says—enough!
Which, in reality, never happens!

To pause, to stop, to restart...
Do we not feel the same
when it comes to life?
To pause, to stop, to restart!
Always so fulfilling
through silent expressions
of a child, a near and dear one—
unknown, yet so known.

The phrase we always hear—
we never need a reason to be happy!

The Living God

He who is in us and outside us,
who beats in every heartbeat,
With *him*, we exist;
in *his* presence, we were born
as one bone and flesh!

Why do we think we are apart
when *he* is in every heart—
the heart of a seeker,
the heart of a lover.
Is *he* not the same everywhere?

Make your heart your guide,
your best friend.
Where the living God resides
he will guide, *he* will speak.
Just surrender unto *him*!

What do you see?
What do you feel?
Can you feel *his* presence within?
Can you hear *him* talking to you?
For *he* is the God within!

Not to be found in
a temple, a church or mosque,
but in everything that exists,

in every living being.
Identify *him*, O frail mind!

He is within, *he* is with us.
Pure as pure can be—
like a newborn babe
free from all bondage
revelling in a loving heart.

Ye fools! Run not, hither thither.
See *him* in all,
worship *him* in all,
see *his* reflection in all!
He is God living amidst us…

Thank God for Mothers

Thank God for mothers!
For she is the reason I exist.
In many ways, is she not God in form?

A form I trust.
A form I revere.
A form I love.
A form connecting me with the formless
with her mere presence.

I end, where I began...
Thank God for mothers!

Contrasts

The bright sparkling sun,
shining in the light blue sky;
the dark cloudy night,
the crescent tinge of a moon
adorning its beauty.

Life is filled with such contrasts—
between siblings,
between lovers,
in everything that is beautiful—
which is evident in nature.

The very design of life
is its varied differences;
in it we have to identify
our very nature—
the purpose of our existence!

Though roads are different,
to reach these destinations,
we realize each journey counts.
They may be bright and beautiful
or dark and dingy…

How you perceive it does not matter.
The first wobbly step of a child,
the races *he* runs thereafter,

the silence within a place of worship
the commotion of a market place...

Each has a way of adding to Self.

Ah! Isn't this what I call a life of contrasts!

The Freedom

The ripples of water,
the sounds of chirping birds,
the rising sun,
the vastness of the universe.

Everything defines freedom.
In nature what we see *is;*
what we do not see *is not.*
This Truth is crystal clear.

In human beings,
this is very different.
What we see, may not be true.
What we feel and believe truly may be.

Freedom to me is that aspect of life
where I am able to feel and believe in,
more than what I can perceive.

In feeling and believing, I become one.
In perceiving, I judge.
It is in feeling
that I feel free…

As free as a lark,
to fly and to soar
high in the sky
without any limitations.

It is through this discovery
I develop the strength
to surpass and surprise,
and to fathom the true meaning of freedom!

Eternal Dance

Dancing
is my sadhana,
a prayer to invoke divinity.
It takes me to another world
where none exist
but me and my God.

O, how I love this
divine communion
where at one moment
he pulls my hair,
teases me, and in another,
stealthily blindfolds my eyes.

Yet, in the next moment
I lose myself in *his* embrace.
He is my Krishna,
my peacock-feathered,
blue-coloured eternal
companion and beloved.

I dance and keep dancing
expressing my emotions,
gradually moving apart

into the unknown...
with one hand in the air,
and the other hand below.

The Sufi whirls, mesmerizing.
The divine connecting the mortal
to the immortal...
Dissolving all imperfections.
Detaching from attachment
but unto the source.

My eternal dance of life
in divine communion found!

Silence

A word intoxicating and pure!

Children in
a Montessori house—
on their own, off by themselves,
so busy, so content
not a word to be heard.

A mere whisper
dissolves into silence…
A delight to the human eye.
A personal experience
as close to feeling God.

Since then, I have longed to go
deep into silence
within, to understand
that stillness means to be quiet.

Learning ever more
to silent the chattering mind.
To be like a child—
Ever peaceful, ever pure.
Dissolving into *his* work or play,
without any worry or care!

Regardless of what the world may think,
gently moving on, in *his* stride.
And in that they pride.
As silence reveals itself in the
sheer innocence of a child!

The Most Powerful Love

Love is when I do not know
where I end and where you begin,
what will draw within, what in my life
I simply need to flow with...

Love is when I am engulfed in
a strange bond with someone
beyond my comprehension.
Yet so complete.

Love is when there is no me
there is no you, it is always
us, we and ours.
It connects me to my inner self.

Love is when I realize God
is the very self in all beings;
it comes through devotion
and I surrender to my God.

Love has no boundaries,
no caste, no creed.
It is all encompassing.
It comes through *his* grace.

Love can never be
explained in mere words.
The energy vibrates within,
to change the world.

Love is when I do not know
how things unfold.
In letting go of my mind, I realize—
the powerful love of the divine has taken over...

A Soul Connection

There never is a day
I live without you.
There never is a moment
I think not of you.

In every breath of mine,
in every heartbeat,
I can feel you;
Yet why do I pine for you?

You and me are never apart,
we are one in soul;
together we laugh, we cry,
we dance, we pray.

A teardrop in your eyes
fills an ocean in mine;
a smile on your lips
makes me ecstatic with joy.

What is this connection, my beloved?
I meet you not, yet I feel?
I am always with you
in thoughts and words.

Every action of mine—
lifting a child, caressing

an abandoned soul—
brings me closer to you!

Distance dissolves into union,
into a soul connection—
indefinable, unfathomable,
eternal,
immortal!

My Flight of Fancy

Flight of fancy takes me takes me up, takes me down.
Sometimes makes me still, sometimes takes me all around.
My imagination like butterfly wings, fluttering gently in the winds.
Are you the flower I rest upon or the colours from the sun long gone?

Dare To Let Go

Stream of life,
keep flowing, keep on and on.
Let go of the past,
march into the present,
await the surprises
the future holds.

Clinging like fetters,
like chains bearing us down,
brings with it boredom.
So why not let go!
To open to a new horizon,
a new way to live life?

Who knows?
A miracle may unfold,
lifting us from a life of
sorrow to joy,
euphoria, exhilaration
bliss, happiness, and more…

Making us realize
that this life
is a cosmic drama.
We have to live it,
rowing this boat
merrily, merrily, merrily…

So, let us affirm
that this is not my will
but Thine.
All we have to do
is let go
and with bliss into eternity flow.

Why Love?

Love transcends all boundaries,
knows not whom to love
knows not why to love,
but loves for it wants to love,
not for fame or applause,
but for the sake of love
and love alone!

A true lover seeks not comfort,
but wants to give
through word and action,
through unimaginable ways
beyond comprehension,
letting the other go on ahead,
because there is no other!

Is it not love when we cry
for the right reason?
When we see someone cry,
a tear trickles down.
When we see another smile,
a smile blossoms on our lips too.
A mere touch dissolves into union!

This is true love.
It transcends all boundaries;
knows not whom

to love and why to love,
but to love and love alone—
for the purpose of love is love.
The passion of a lover is love!

My Inner World

The beauty in a picture is
in its completeness.
The charm in an individual
is *his* personality,
in *his* core,
reflecting on *his* face,
through *his* twinkling eyes.

We are born to blossom.
We are born to be legends,
to do ordinary things in
the most extraordinary ways.
It depends entirely on us—
how we use ourselves
or lose ourselves in the world!

True beauty is to go within,
to ask for existential grace,
in whatever we do;
to explore the inner world,
in which entirety exists.
To see a painting and wonder
'Aha! How beautiful this is!'

So why not seek for quietude
to feel God within,
the one who reveals us to us,

who takes us into the world within
where true beauty beholds
and shows us an inner world
where we can all seek *him*!

Whispers From Eternity

The chirping of birds,
the splashing of waves,
the rising and setting sun.

The roar of a lion,
the wail of a child,
the lullaby sung by a mother—
every sound resonates within me
—playing and repeating itself
as beautifully strung notes.

Silence conveys enough,
more than words do,
and we learn to connect with each other.

All differences dissolve
as we feel absolved
and experience the bliss of love.

In this blissful state,
we feel one with all
and peace descends.

Ego vanishes,
happiness manifests,
and wisdom reveals
something beyond words,
beyond thought and action,
where love and happiness prevails…

In Search of God

Holy Eternity, boundless Glory,
I crave to invoke Thee.
I know not how and who art Thou?
Are you a perennial flow,
the source of all existence,
or art Thou just like me?

Can I separate me from you?
Are you and me made from One?
Or do I distance myself from you,
when I seek you out there,
in the transient nature of the world!

Pray! Remove this fettered self,
let me be with Thee without hindrances.

Pray! Show me the way through confusion,
to never ask for anything but
to seek answers within.

The world cannot hinder one
who is connected...
As evil ceases to exist
in the eyes of the one who sees Thee in all,
hatred disappears when
only love exists in all who love.

The Child Within

Young or old,
are we all not like children,
emotional, crying
for things we do not get,
weeping of expectations unmet,
and setbacks in relationships?

My mind takes me back
to my childhood,
playing with all the memories
in my mind's eye,
like a movie unnamed—
undefinable, yet so precious.

I recall a child so happy,
laughing, playing, frolicking,
for no reason at all;
asking her grandfather,
'What did you do when you
were as young as me, Grandpa?'
'Did you have many friends?'
'Were you naughty too?'
'Did you help your parents?'

Pausing awhile, winking and smiling,
filled with excitement, *he* says,
'I was very naughty.'

'I once pushed a girl into the well
in our village... I spilt some oil on the
floor and tried to swim in it.'
With twinkling eyes,
the child says, 'Oh!'

She rushes inside, brings a big bucket
of water, throws it on the floor,
and starts swimming in it,
squealing with joy, with bliss!

Here is the child within!

Love

What is love?
Can it ever be explained?
Will words do it justice?
Is it temporary or permanent?

Many a time I have attempted
to describe love,
yet when I try to express it,
I am unable to put it into words!

It is but a feeling that takes me
on a high in the beginning,
and gradually seems to diminish,
if not nurtured well enough.

The purest form of love is
between a mother and a child,
between the devotee and God.

A love which only cleanses,
purifies the subtlest corner
within, drops all expectations,
except wanting to give and keep
giving, receiving nothing in return.

A lover loves for love alone,
feels a deep connection
in the solitude of the heart
with another soul.

The power of love
fills a being with
happiness, peace and strength,
and they transcend the fetters holding them in!

Loss

Loss is to be deprived
of what? Love, feelings?
Emotions and thoughts?
Gestures and words?

Out is to remove
unwanted clutter from within,
expelling it, never to return
and then, to experience freedom!

Someone, some thoughts
predominantly prevail
in the inner chambers.
The subconscious mind lingering on!

Special people we miss
when they can no more
be at our side in this journey
of life, which is nothing
but a cosmic play!

Loss of someone special
brings tears to the eyes
silences all words...
and connects me to the divine!

Hope Not

When God blesses us,
when God touches us,
everything that we do,
everything that we touch,
is tinged with *his* blessing.
If we have found this within,
we now carry it everywhere.

In hope, we assign desires,
start expecting returns.
When we hope not, we
deeply surrender to God
to take us through, even if
we make blunders,
we fall down and err.

All we know is there is a Hand
which guides us,
unseen, abstract, yet
ours and only ours.
It stops us from being crushed,
strengthens us to peace,
and fills the void within.

A grain of God's blessing
is enough to fill this life,
with joy unparalleled,

with ecstasy divine.
The one thing I hope for
is to receive *his* grace;
the one which is entirely mine.

Love the Living

I watch thee gaze through the sky
as the sun sheds its radiance
on the external self.

I hear thy whisper through the
silence of the earth,
as I leave my footprints on sand.

I feel thy touch as the wind
gently caresses and takes
away my unwanted burdens.

I smell thy fragrance through the waves,
which splash over and cleanse me,
washing away my ignorance.

I taste thy love through the fiery red
sparks of fire,
filling me with a zest for life!

My Cup of Tea

My tea—
I love sipping my cup of tea, early in the morning.
I sit in the garden and gaze at the blue skies.
Cinnamon, clove, mint and milk. Peace and bliss!
I love the act of drinking tea.
I say, my tea is nothing short of magic!

Red

Red adorns the hands of a dancer,
as she sways and moves gracefully;
a stage to enthrall the audience,
with her vibrant pirouettes.

A Kathak dancer she,
her footsteps aflame within.
A colour, so red
so bright and beautiful.

She and her elegant attire
whirl and twirl endlessly
like a Sufi dancer trained to love
her beloved.

And Peace Became Me

Melodious notes of the flute
fill me with ecstasy.
Pray, quench my soul's thirst!
Where are you, my Krishna?
Play not hide and seek.

Morning beckons sweetness,
as the sky fills with music
falling from Thy divine lips!
Who are you, my Krishna?
Unseen, yet so near.

The fresh breeze
caresses my sore cheeks
longing for Thy holy touch!
What are you, my Krishna?
A feeling, a sensation, bliss.

Stream of life's longing
merges into the ocean—
endless, infinite, unfathomable!
Why are you so, my Krishna?
Incomprehensible, indefinable.

Plucking flowers as offerings,
stringing garlands with tulsi,
as if in wedlock, a bride!

Which form are you, my Krishna?
A devotee, a seeker or none.

The self does not exist
in your everlasting presence.
My immense love only questions!
How are you so, my Krishna?
Making me merge into oblivion!

Thou Art Divine

O Being! Thou art divine!
Thou art made in the image of
God to love, and only love!

Why fear? Why expect remorse?
When Thy nature is to love
and only love.
In love there is no self,
there is no I,
there is all pervading oneness.

Feel the peace within,
feel the peace without.
Close your eyes and feel *him,*
percolating in every breath,
dancing through every cell,
the rhythmic heartbeat of *his.*

O Being! Thou art Divine!
Thou art made in the image of
God to love and only love!

Bliss In Surrender

To dance, to love, to rejoice
in the arms of the divine,
leaving us without a choice!

To fantasize, to dream, to lose
in the lap of our beloved
fills us with joy immense!

To bathe, to drench, to dissolve
in thoughts of the saviour
etches us with a new stroke!

To evolve, to create, to grow
in the presence of our master
recharges us with a fresh glow!

To hope, to think, to fathom
in our connection with the creator
kindles within a magical passion!

To forbear, to contemplate, to desire
in the grace of our protector
awakens the mind higher!

To ignite, to spark, to arouse
in the radiance of the nurturer
lights a fire without much heat!

To dance, to love, to rejoice
in the arms of the divine.
Are we left with a choice?

The Dreamy Eyes

Dreamy eyes—
so mesmerizing, cool, lost;
mistaken as a fool, lost in *his* own cocoon.

But what meaning does life hold without these dreamy eyes?
When one beholds not what is, but what could be!

Hey, my dreamy eyes, let's make them come true; let's rise!

Thou Art Near

In every leaf,
in every flower art thou;
in every heartbeat,
in every breath art thou.
Why go here and there
when thou art so near?

In every atom,
in every cell art thou;
in every pain,
in my sorrow art thou.
Why go here and there
when thou art so near?

In the twilight,
in the dusk art thou;
in my joy,
in my bliss art thou.
Why go here and there
when thou art so near?

In every spark
of the fire art thou;
in my warmth,
in my depth art thou.
Why search here and there,
go within when thou art so near?

In the waves
of the ocean art thou;
in the highs,
in the downs art thou.
Why sail here and there
when thou art so near?

Celebrations Galore

The festival of Holi
fills the heart with joy.
Red, yellow, blue, green—
luminous, magnificent colours
spread across the horizon.

Through the silence of the
universe, some notes echo—
jiggity jig jiggity jig jig jig
he he he he he he hee,
And lo! Appear three minions.

A mischief or a prank
sparks their hearts,
water, colour, balloons
spread all around
that is all we adore!

Here comes the water pistol
the water balloons,
splashing the backs
of passers-by treading along
unaware, unknown on the road!

He he he he he he hee!
Jiggity jig jiggity jig jig jig!
These are the sounds we hear

from these three little ones
frolicking, chatting, jumping!

What next, what more
can we do to have fun?
It is Holi, after all.
It comes once a year
dance, rejoice and fall!

We will not spare anyone—
drench all, colour all.
It is Holi, after all.
It comes once a year
dance, rejoice and fall!

Beings Of Divinity

The sun shines on us,
the tree gives us shade,
the birds chirp away.

Nature in its vastness
bestows us with abundance,
and in its wrath, reveals
something awry.

As a being of divinity
what is our innate nature?
Love, peace and harmony!

But alas! we move away.
Desires, expectations,
achievements, overpowering
our conscious self.

We no more see,
we no more feel,
we no more hear.

As the eyes behold a sight,
as the heart feels beauty,
as words touch the soul,
as hands express love!

Sheer garments of divinity
take us closer to the being.
In love, peace and harmony!

In That Moment, I Awakened!

The vastness of the sky;
my immense potential.

The tenderness of the flower;
my mother's touch.

The uniqueness of each leaf;
a special rare self.

The restless waves of the sea;
my wandering mind.

The rootedness of the trunk;
my faith and belief.

God is and God alone *is*.
Now, forever and for eternity!

Why worry, why be anxious?
Feel the peace within.

Why carry such wrath, why hate?
Feel the love in every moment.

Why compare, why compete?
Feel at one, amidst each difference.

Why oscillate, why rush?
Feel the stillness in between.

Why run here, why flee there?
Feel consoled in surrender unto *him*!

As God is and God alone is.
Now, forever and for eternity!

Big Yellow Underwear

The big yellow pair of underwear
hanging out to dry,
washed, cleaned inner-wear,
would anyone like to try?

A tear here, a tear there,
underwear is hard to beat,
a stitch in time with care
will make it once again complete.

A young boy's possession,
an old man's need,
what is there to question?
It is necessity, not greed.

Hidden under a chair,
children use it for their mischief;
the old man is in despair,
wipes his brow with a kerchief.

The big yellow pair of underwear
is indeed a gift to possess,
for it covers that which is bare,
and spares us from the mess!

Speaking to the young prankster,
the old man wants to say,
'Don't treat my underwear as a toy,
for you too shall age, one day!'

Why Complain?

Has not the earth taken all
the fiery blows upon itself
from time immemorial?
Revealing, that we too
bear the same resistance.

Has not the vastness of the sky
always retained its serenity?
The quality of peace and bliss,
an expanse of infinity,
showing us our very nature.

Has not water quenched all
our worries and anxieties?
Nourishing us with the clarity
of thought and vision,
filling our lives with abundance.

Has not fire taught us
to value life in many ways?
Burning all the evil within,
relinquishing our desires
in the flames of purity.

Has not the wind shown us
that we too can get blown away?
We must be mindful
with our words and actions
in this life of delusions!

Peacefully Yours

Everything emanates from *him*.
Everything dissolves in *him*.
What are we?
Who are we?
We know not,
Yet, we always feel a hand
which carries us!

Peace fills the entire being
as we feel one with the creator,
one with creation!
The one and only desire is to feel
him within, feel *him* with.
Pulsating with every
heartbeat, with every breath!

Everything is possible for one
who is connected with *him*,
who is aligned to the laws of life!
For 'tis a joyous ride of ups and downs,
of lows and highs, of going beyond
the imaginary finishing line
where abundance awaits.

The unknown is waiting to
unite with the known,
nothing seems impossible.

Everything is possible.
'I am possible.
I am *he*; *he* is me.'
We are part of this whole.

The entirety of the universe is in
this whole; here, the complete
finds completeness in
the incomplete and rejoices in
everything that is life.
Everything is *his* masterpiece.

We are simply *his* fragments...

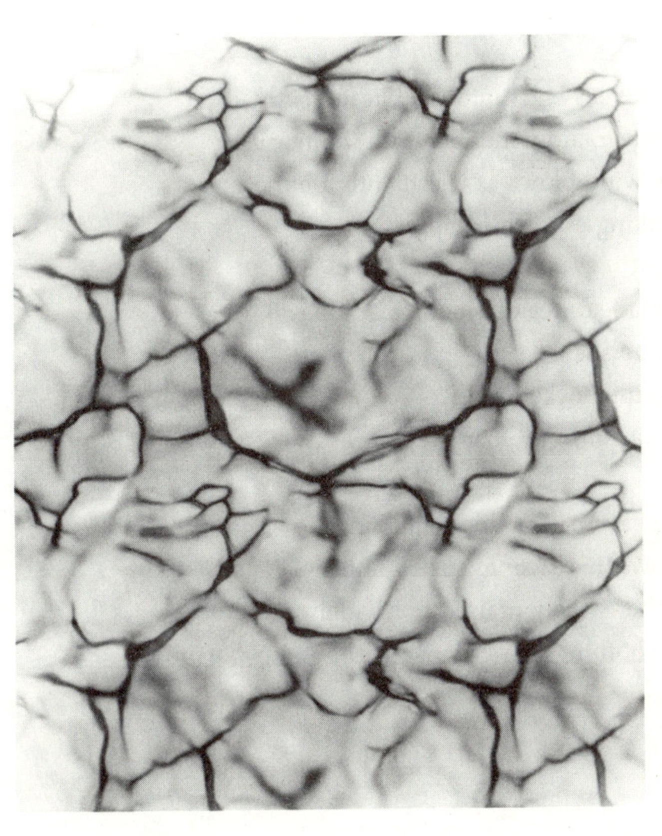

Stillness of The Sea

In the blue sky, floats a multitude of clouds—
white, black, blue, formed of many shades.
An orange sun is about to say farewell
to the evening sky, covered with streaks of red.

The river bends into the ocean gently—
swiftly, rapidly merging into immensity.
The wind blows as it lists into a hurricane,
breaking everything apart.

Myriad scenes of God's creation—
a huge snake, a strong lion,
a couple locked in love—
all vanish in the dark vapoury sky.

As peace dawns upon all beings,
below the sea sings varied notes of music—
neither widely praised nor widely acclaimed,
yet soothing in a cadence without any harshness.

The Little Cloud Said Hello!

My friend, my little cloud.
I watch you as you float
in your soft white dress
through the sky, which is your address.
Watching you, I must confess,
out the window goes my stress!
For you are so happy and free,
Come, drop in for a cup of tea?

A Cosmic Play

In the blue sky,
birds keep flying high.
What freedom, what abandon
as they soar up without a cry!

In the deep ocean,
fishes keep swimming low.
What freedom, what joy
as they go deeper and deeper below!

In the consciousness of the mind,
thoughts keep swarming.
Where God is our one sole refuge
in bliss, peace and quietude!

In an educational institute,
youth keep coming in and out,
classes go on, hands are raised—
sometimes about science, math or art!

In a busy restaurant,
French fries keep selling at a height,
chattering noises, kept at bay
as cozy smiles fill the breezy night!

In the terrace of the house,
clothes keep drying, floating away,
shorts, underwear on the sway,
as the wind enjoys its play!

A Bakery

A picture on the wall
of a ship very small,
Tom Sawyer with a helmet
in the twilight of a pelmet.

Hot bread in the making,
while cookies are baking.
They smell so delicious,
let's make something nutritious.

A song orchestrated,
life is demonstrated,
to keep flowing with the flow
God helps all who glow.

Sitting in a bakery shop,
young kids, talking non-stop,
where the wise and foolish are all alike,
Just like a robber and a spendthrift on a hike.

All eating and simply waiting.
A scene worth a painting.
Smiles and laughter on the rise,
as buddies savour cheese and pies!

The Journey of My Life

A speck of dust was I.
God created me and placed me
in my mother's womb,
to be nurtured and cared for
nine months.
Until born, until I could walk
on my two little feet
and keep growing—from zero
to a young girl, of nine or ten.

The prime years of a child,
the transition to adolescence,
the big leap into adulthood.
I was a witness to all the fun—
running, playing, dancing,
fighting, pranking, snacking—
some of my favourite
chores, leave alone aspiring
to be one among many more.

As I marched into my twenties,
careers were aplenty;
I had to choose what was trendy.
A question oft came to my mind:
why not do something unassigned?
Which resonates with the heart
and not the mind, which touches the soul

of the poor and rich alike?
In that, find a soul mate who is right!

The most profound age
as a woman, as a mother
in her thirties,
maturing with each experience
discovering unconditional love.
Love which keeps growing by giving,
and shrinks by demanding.
A moment here, a moment there.
Isn't life eternally flowing?

Laughter And Tears

Seeing a newborn sleep,
tears dissolve into laughter,
and laughter dissolves into tears...

Communing in silence with my God,
tears dissolve into laughter,
and laughter dissolves into tears...

Connecting the mortal to the divine,
tears dissolve into laughter,
and laughter dissolves into tears...

In the whirling dance of the mystic Sufi,
tears dissolve into laughter,
and laughter dissolves into tears...

Laughter and tears,
faith and fears—this is what I call a beautiful life!

The Drop Became the Ocean

Who am I?
What am I?
Where do I come from?
Which particle do I belong to?
How do I define myself?

Are questions pervading
the inner being?
Unable to comprehend
the answers it is seeking,
knowing something is coming!

Sitting under a tree,
gazing at the lush green lawn,
looking above for a glimpse
of the blue sky and the clouds.

Sitting near the beach,
gazing at the vast depths of water
seems like an endless expanse
of the immense blue ocean.

A flood of answers gush
into the being, filling me
with immense joy, bliss abounding
as a realization dawns!

I am the drop of water,
which merges into the ocean.
I am a particle of the Formless,
which merges into the Form
I come from *him*, my Source!

How can I define myself?
When I am only *him*.
I come from *him* and dissolve
in *him*—that is all I know.
I am nothing without *him*!

Sleep

Aha! The bliss to close the eyes.
Aha! The peace it brings to the mind.
To drift into a world where none exist,
detached from all,
connected only to what is within—
in a dreamland of its own making.

Sleep to refresh the body, mind and the soul...

And It Rained Blessings

The gentle touch of *his* hand,
the snuggle into *his* embrace,
the mystical sound of *his* voice,
the rapture it caused within.
For a moment, everything was still
and I knew not where I was...

The stars and moon above,
the glimmering and shining glow,
the quietude of the night,
the rapture it caused within.
For a moment, everything was still
and I knew not where I was...

The magic land we talk about,
the words that touch the heart,
the lips that trill into a song,
the rapture it causes within.
For that moment, everything is still
and I know not where I am...

In that moment, I experience it all;
in the nothingness, I gain
a ball, an eternal dance of souls.
I realize there is no rapture,
but a stillness in every capture
as it rains in blessings...

The blessings of the divine,
the blessings of a force,
the blessings of a mystic,
which rains and keeps
raining for me to realize
It had rained blessings…

Faith Was, Faith Is, Faith Will Be

Ah, the quiet and blissful hour,
hour of union and fulfillment,
hour of joy ever complete.
It makes me empty yet full—
with what, I know not...

I dream of a moment that unites
me with Thee
to make me believe that faith was.

Ah, the quiet blissful hour,
hour of union and fulfillment,
hour of joy ever complete.
It fills me and keeps me full
to sing songs that no one has ever sung.

To think thoughts that never before have come,
to walk a path that none have tread—
to me, that is faith, faith is...

Ah, the quiet blissful hour,
hour of union and fulfillment,
hour of joy ever complete.
To love all with love that no one has felt,
to give peace to all for whom no peace has existed.

Flowing tears of bhakti at the feet of God—
to me, that is faith, faith is...
To me, faith will be, will forever be.

Faith Begins With Me

Faith, ah, faith! It begins with me.
Moments come, phases pass by,
yet there has never been a second
in my life where I have not held on to
faith—it begins with me.

Faith is in believing in myself.
Faith is in introspecting within.
Faith is unseen yet the closest.
Faith keeps me going, keeps me flowing.
As faith, ah, faith! It begins with me.

Faith surrounds me like a whirlpool
as I keep swimming and dissolving
in this magnificent aura of bliss.
Faith fills me with immense joy.
As faith, ah, faith! It begins with me.

I discover the magical world of faith;
I can face anything in trusting *him*;
He is the formless presence
who resides within me and fills me
with faith. Ah, faith! It begins with me.

As I go deeper and deeper into my faith
I realize it has no beginning, no end.
It is the only anecdote I share.

A well-deserved happiness found in loving life.
As faith, ah, faith! Faith is above. Faith is in God!

I hold on to my God with faith.
I love my God with unquestionable resolve.
I surrender unto my God with unflinching faith.
Faith begins with me.
Faith engulfs every being in its aura!

Miracle

Miracle!
A word so subtle,
a feeling so intricate,
a thought so deep.

It fills the very being
with magical moments,
moments which take me
into a trance.

Awakening a desire
to forget, forgive and move on
As I feel life is transient—
everything will finally pass on...

To experience a miracle
I must hold a belief,
believe in a force infinite
which carries, ignites and holds on...

In the very word
is something incomprehensible—
nothing seems to exist and
all are fleeting moments—

yet, the miracle!
A word so very subtle,
a feeling so intricate,
a thought so deep.

Nature

Everything in nature lures me
teaches me to endure,
shows me the path to greatness,
to follow a pattern with sincerity.

The sun, the moon, the sky,
the trees, the plants, the flowers,
the ocean, the rivers, the streams,
the mountains, the horizons, the birds—

all flow in a rhythm, the rhythm of life
I too am inspired to flow in rhythm.
What stops me, what breaks the flow?
What makes the intellect contemplate so?

I feel a lack of discipline,
the zeal to give back to nature,
what has been given in abundance
to hold on to these key attributes—

to believe in my own potential,
tap into my inner resources.
To identify my inner nature that
sets me apart as an individual!

Clouds

The white and blue clusters,
the shapes and sizes they form;
everything about the clouds
so real, so very palpable!

Something undefinable,
something beyond expression.

I talk to them, I express to them,
I see a loved one in them,
I see something unseen,
I hear the sounds of thunder!

For me, it is my God
who is always there!

I can make a form in those clusters.
I can see the formless in those clusters.
I am always protected.
I feel *he* always has *his* eyes on me!

What beauty, what charm!
I am *his* child, *his* very own.

I surrender unto *his* might,
I lose myself in *his* sight,
I dissolve the self on this night,
as I feel *his* embrace, so very tight!

The Feminine Touch

O woman! Woman! Woman!
How tender and merciful
can you be?
Spreading your fragrance
of love and happiness
without ever thinking of me?

Have you never felt what
it would be to receive?
How unconditionally can you
give, and keep giving?
Never once thinking
about what it feels like to just be?

In this world, where we are
groomed to bear and bear all
as a woman, have you never
felt a sense of loss
in letting go of your identity?
And for men to take the call!

'No.' An answer arises from
a space unknown and uncommon
to all, but open to those
pure at heart; women
who appear weak, but are blessed
with the spirit of a caged lioness within.

We are made to compliment
the ones who run the tribe;
we term them men.
They, with their outer strength,
become the architects of the world
while we bring forth new life!

It is this feminine touch
that encompasses all
with love, tender care and bliss,
spreading its fragrance to
one and all, without any
bias, prejudice or acclaim.

O woman! Woman! Woman!
How tender and merciful
can you be?
Spreading your fragrance
of love and happiness
through the lives of so many!

The Day I Found My Wings

I closed my eyes and saw the skies.
I could feel myself floating through the air,
blue-white clusters of clouds
like spies around me.

Dim, opalescent infinity spread
came and took me away,
I zoomed through an open space
enamoured by a mysterious ether.

Left, right, north, south, above, below—
I found no landing.
I spun through limitlessness,
I whirled through the eternal banks of life.

Bit by bit, my mental chariot melted.
Decked with lights of subtle vision,
there seemed an awakening of an unknown kind...
Unfathomed miracles!

My body had dissolved into the air,
my thoughts had burnt in pure light
into an all-transmuting flame
of an unknown sort. I delight.

Ah! I had found my wings to fly
into eternity, through the myriad stars.

With the waking of the dawn,
I attempt to be the shepherd of stray souls.

Yet, be one among the clouds,
adorned with rainbow garlands,
floating on the tides of space,
to emotionally surge over the sea of all beings.

I will sing through the voices of all,
I will commune through silent prayers,
I will love all with the love of God.
For I had found my wings to fly!

The Love of a Son

The love of a son is as deep as an ocean;
the depths of which cannot be seen, only felt.
As a phrase explains,
silent waters
flow deep within...
So it is when it comes to the love of a son!

I Existed No More

Sitting in the seat of silence,
I lost myself in my Lord.
Seconds passed into minutes,
minutes into hours, and
I existed no more.

Waking to the rising sun,
I lost myself in its radiant rays.
Seconds passed into minutes,
minutes into hours, and
I existed no more.

Experiencing the chirping of birds,
I lost myself in their sweet melody.
Seconds passed into minutes,
minutes into hours, and
I existed no more.

Walking near the shore of the beach,
I dissolved myself in the waves.
Seconds passed into minutes,
minutes into hours, and
I existed no more.

Dancing in surrender to dance,
I lost myself in divine ecstasy.
Seconds passed into minutes,

minutes into hours, and
I existed no more.

Gazing at the sky from my window,
I felt myself floating through the clouds.
Seconds passed into minutes,
minutes into hours, and
I, indeed, existed no more.

What is it to exist?
I sometimes feel this way.
Nothing beyond, nothing within—
All that is seems a void
So why say, I exist no more?

From where does this self come from?
Sheer ego and self-centredness.
When there is nothing but the one
in whom one dissolves to become one.
To exist no more.

A Flight Without Fetters

As I soared, higher and higher
in the inner plane of consciousness,
I felt the sheer joy of flying.

It was a flight without fetters,
an ascent upwards,
dropping chains
of belief and superstition.
A quest to achieve freedom!

Freedom is a rather naïve concept,
fit to those most divine—
Oh, to set oneself free from limits,
explore the external world,
and seek resoluteness within.

Then why do I bind myself in
petty thoughts, in fear and control?
All I should do is fly!
Fly high—higher—highest.
Discover the true self within
where no limitlessness exists,
where thoughts are firm and smooth.

Eternal strife for freedom
to see good in all and help all,
to see good within and beyond all.

My flight of fancy I choose to call it!

It is a world of love and kindness,
where selflessness flourishes,
where perfection has no limits,
where peace, love and kindness thrive!

I keep soaring higher and higher.
In my inner plane of consciousness,
feeling the sheer joy of flight!

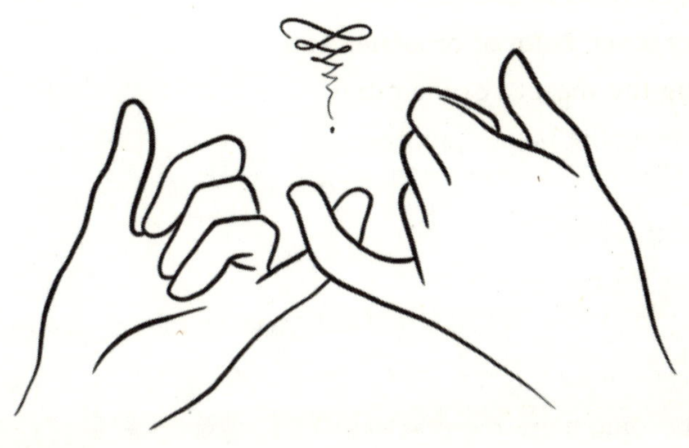

A Beautiful Life

A beautiful life!
Sitting beside the river bank,
splashing water on each other,
lying in the lap of nature,
gazing high up in the sky.

A beautiful life!
Walking hand in hand,
with a lover, beloved or a friend,
feeling the warmth of the other,
dissolving the pain of another.

A beautiful life!
Ah, isn't it beautiful?
When God becomes the divine lover,
we cease to be a giver,
and become mere receptacles.

Receivers of *his* divine grace,
receivers of blessings infinite.
When receiving fades away
and giving becomes a new way of life...
A beautiful life, isn't it?

A Friend

A friend is one without a second;
a friend is with determination;
a friend is one who surpasses expectation;
a friend comes from a land of compassion.

No caste, no creed, no sex, no religion
can define a friend; a friend is simply a friend,
merely accepting
as the bond goes beyond any explanation.

It is said that we choose our friends.
But I believe a heart connects with another
and the hearts feel for one another.
For sure, being a friend is like no other!

A Mystical Night

The sky had turned dark,
the moon was shining bright;
I wondered how to be a lark
to soar high with all my might.

The night had revealed
a secret beyond my imagination.
Perhaps, something I had dreamt of,
which had never surfaced before.

Nature has its mystical ways,
to entice, excite and enthuse
the beholder—who always prays
to the Supreme, to have a say!

A voice from within shrieks,
with joy, with bliss and poise,
rejoicing the fall of each day,
as it turns into night, all gay!

The sky had turned dark,
the stars were shining bright;
I felt I was soaring like a lark
to conquer human plight.

The marvel of something so deep,
deeper than a star,

went beyond every bar
to rise, higher, much higher.

As I was soaring high into a plane
beyond, deeper into the unknown,
the sky had turned red
and the sun was about to rise!

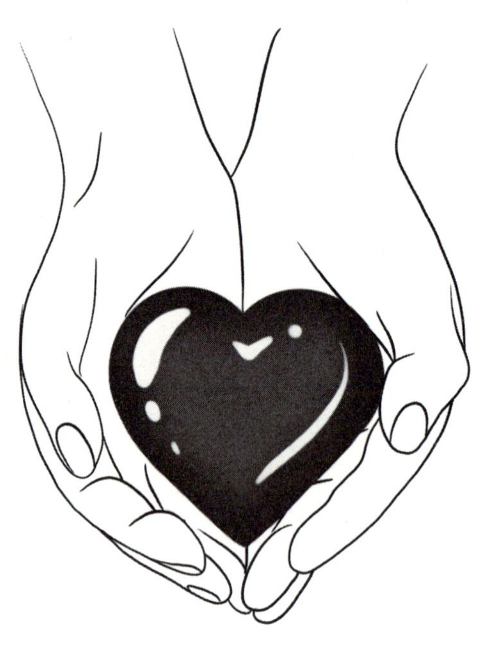

Faith

Faith works!
Faith alone works!
Let the stream of love
flow into the soul unbarred.
This alone will fill us with life.

Hinder it not through fear,
block it not with petty thoughts.
Let it flow its normal course.
It alone will wash and clean,
it alone will revive and redeem.

Faith works!
Faith alone works!
It will bring life and loveliness.
It will bring peace and happiness,
as the stream of love flows on.

Unhindered and unblocked by fear,
fear exists not in faith,
experiences no inner storm,
save the flow to flow on and on and on...
to face anything in trusting *him*!

Finding Myself in the Chaos

Life paves the way for a resolute soul,
they say, but who am I?
Where do I belong?
What is my destination?
These are the questions that invade
my mind, my heart, my very being!

When I gaze at the sky,
the moonlight shines upon me.
I feel like I am being cleansed.
I am being purified,
basking in this divine love.
Does the moon not signify love?

Surely, it does.
It always has
for eternity.
The moon signifies love, the meeting of souls
who have been apart and away,
in different parts of the world.

On a moonlit night, love unites.
The union of souls paves the way
for a resolute soul to seek
the destination, to unite with God,
to connect with all,
to realize that I too am significant!

Whether it is to find myself in chaos
or feel that there is no chaos in reality—
'tis simply a figment of my imagination.
Lo! Ah! At that instance I drop
this from within, from without—
and merge with the cosmos, my home...

Divine Love

I am made in the image of God
to love all and love always.
Where does this love come from?
It comes from true love.
I realize that I must think,
speak, feel and act.
It comes from God.

He is ever within me,
inspiring and guiding me.
Why should there be nervousness?
Why must chaos intrude?
Flashes of divine joy come to me
when I unite my within with God.

The power of God's love sweeps in
like an ocean, surging through the heart, cleansing as it floods.
It purifies me, it takes me deeper within.
As this can only be attained in silence,
I quieten the mind
as an offering at the altar of my God;
my prayer unto him.

It is only in this surrender that I realize that this body is
a little bubble of his divine energy
in his cosmic sea.
So where is the chaos?
There is only divine love!

I Stand Tall as a Woman

In God's divine kingdom,
there is no man or woman.
We are all alike in blood and flesh,
so where does the difference arise?

When I separate myself from
my God, my centre, from my root
which connects me to my core,
where lies the consciousness of my God.

Then, I realize I have moved away...
I have drifted away into the material world
where a man and a woman are seen as separate,
but in reality are we apart?

I have never felt it to be so,
not that it is the truth—
though I have taken birth in a family
with four elder brothers who have made me feel like it's true.

Yet once there was a revelation!
Nothing hence has been the same.
Creed, caste, sex, religion, all discrimination
dissolved as I felt drenched in love.

The love I speak about
is not ordinary but beyond

imagination; once tasted
all other tastes cease to exist...

Divine love.
A love that makes me lose sleep,
a love that makes me forget the self,
a love that drops the self into the all.

Then, how do I say I stand tall as a woman?
I see not a man or a woman but all.
All I feel is this beautiful human birth
to prove my worth as a being of God's creation.

A being that radiates love,
a being that fills all lives with love,
a being that paints this canvas of life
to make everyone feel loved and loved.

I realize this birth is a gift from God
to become a gift unto the world!
Every thought, word and action, emanates
from the love of God and I keep loving...

I am a human being
living life as it is worth, designed by my Master
to emanate bliss,
to stand tall as a divine being of love!

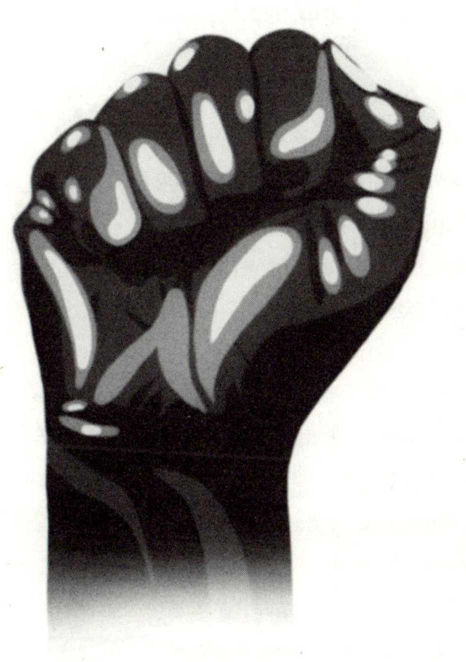

It Was Not Easy, But I Did It

Lift yourself, by yourself;
Only you can do it.
Nothing in life is easy.
If it is easy, it is not life.
If easy, life ceases and death prevails.

A challenge-free death is possible,
but a challenge-free life can never be.
So why even think of having one?
Unflinching faith is possible,
conviction in the self upheld high!
So bounce back, be big.
Nothing can stop you.

It is in moments of darkness
that stars are found.
It is in moments of darkness
that one sees the shining sun.
It is the eyes that we have to seek
by surrendering to a higher force.
God's delays are not denials.

As I rose from deep slumber,
the words of a child resonated,
the words of my God reverberated,
the embrace of my source filled me.
I had never felt as secure as I felt today;

the faith I had held on to
was now carrying me in *his* arms.

What more, what next?
Where from, where next?
I knew I had a larger mission,
I knew my vision was pure.
To fill all lives with happiness
from all that I had endured...
To stop not and go on and on.

I knew it would not be easy,
but I did it! I lifted myself,
by myself; so let me help others too.
If it is easy, it is not life.
If easy, life ceases and death prevails.